How to Be Friends with a Dragon

Valeri Gorbachev

ALBERT WHITMAN & COMPANY
Chicago, Illinois

Simon loved dragons.
He loved dragon toys.

He loved books
about dragons,

and drawing dragons.

In fact, he loved *everything* about dragons.

"Do you want to know a secret?" Simon asked his sister, Emma.

"Sure," said Emma.

"I want to make friends with a dragon," said Simon.

"Well," said Emma. "If you want to make friends with a dragon, you must remember the rules…"

"If you ever meet a dragon, don't show that you are scared of him."

"OK," said Simon. "But I won't be scared."

"And don't try to scare him,"
said Emma.

"OK," Simon agreed. "I won't."

"You should try to be nice to the dragon," Emma said. "Then maybe he'll invite you to his castle."

"I will give him a big bunch of flowers," said Simon.

"You know, you'll be the dragon's guest, so you better behave yourself," said Emma. "Don't swing on the dragon's tail and don't hop on the stairs."

"I got it," Simon said.

"When the dragon shows you pictures
of his ancestors, don't say they look
frightening," said Emma.

"Of course I won't!"
cried Simon. "I love
pictures of dragons!"

"Don't act surprised when the dragon fries a few eggs in his mouth. After all, dragons can breathe fire," said Emma.

"OK," said Simon.

"And don't forget to say 'thank you' for lunch," said Emma.

"I won't forget," said Simon.

"After lunch, when the dragon takes a nap, you really shouldn't try to wake him up by putting a stick into his nose," said Emma.

"Why not?" asked Simon. "Don't you think he'd like a little joke?"

"It's not a good idea to play jokes on a dragon. Dragons don't just breathe fire, they SNEEZE fire!" said Emma.
"I understand," said Simon.

"After his nap, if the dragon takes you flying on his back, don't forget to wear your seatbelt," said Emma.

"OK," said Simon. "I won't forget."

"And don't even *think* of bringing that dragon to school to introduce him to your friends," Emma said.

"That's too bad because I am sure they would love to meet him. But it's OK. I won't," said Simon.

"I'll just play with the dragon
in my room, all by myself.
I'm sure he'll love
my toys."

"Oh no!" said Emma. "And don't you dare bring that dragon to our house. He's way too big to get into your room."

"But I really want the dragon to say good night to me."

"I'm sure he will," said Emma. "If you follow all the rules."

"OK," said Simon. "I promise…"

" . . .At least, I'll try."

For Christopher

Text and illustrations copyright © 2012 by Valeri Gorbachev.
Published in 2012 by Albert Whitman & Company.

Printed in China.
10 9 8 7 6 5 4 3 BP 16 15 14 13 12

Designed by Patrick Collins

Library of Congress Cataloging-in-Publication Data
Gorbachev, Valeri.
How to be friends with a dragon / written and illustrated by Valeri Gorbachev.
 p.   cm.
Summary: A girl tells her younger brother all of the rules he must follow in order to befriend a dragon.
ISBN 978-0-8075-3432-8
[1. Dragons—Fiction. 2. Brothers and sisters—Fiction. 3. Behavior—Fiction.] I. Title.
PZ7.G6475How 2012   [E]—dc22   2011008566

For more information about Albert Whitman & Company,
please visit our web site at www.albertwhitman.com.